TREASURE SEEKERS

TREASURE SEEKERS

Published by Barking Frog
an imprint of BHC Press

Library of Congress Control Number:
2018930006

ISBN: 978-1-947727-27-4

Also available in ebook

Visit the publisher at:
www.bhcpress.com

OTHER BOOKS IN

THE
CHILDHOOD LEGENDS®
SERIES

BY JUDITH BLEVINS & CARROLL MULTZ

Operation Cat Tale

One Frightful Day

Blue

The Ghost of Bradbury Mansion

White Out

A Flash of Red

Back in Time

Coming Soon

Summer Vacation

Part 1: Castaways
Part 2: Blast-off

TABLE OF CONTENTS

AUTHORS' NOTE

"The adventures of the $R^*U^*1^*2s$, as chronicled in The Childhood Legends Series®, have taken us down memory lane," one elderly reader said recently. "Your childhood novels mirror many incidents I experienced growing up," another said. "Life hasn't changed much since I was a kid," a ninety-six-year-old fan said, holding up our latest young adult novel.

Realizing that our young adult books were being enjoyed as much by adults as our targeted audience, we have been taking heed of topics of interest to both the young and old alike. When we were asked not long ago why there was no "finding buried treasure" novel in the series, we knew we had no choice but to make that our next effort.

Whether finding a pot of gold at the end of the rainbow or winning the lottery, your treasure is just around the corner. It might not be one of the two mentioned, and is likely one already received but not recognized. Whatever the treasure you seek, we hope you find it. And when you do, make it work miracles not only in your life but in the lives of others—much like it did for the $R^*U^*1^*2s$ in the novel you are about to read.

As usual, our thanks to Margie Vollmer Rabdau and BHC Press for their editing skills and technical assistance. Our special thanks to our publisher, BHC Press for taking The Childhood Legends Series® to a whole new level.

TO OUR INSPIRATION

*Cole, Emily, Joey, Kate, Kirsten,
Logan, Taran, Trenton, Bridget,
Hannah, Irina and Caroline.*

THE
CHILDHOOD LEGENDS®
SERIES

TREASURE SEEKERS

BY JUDITH BLEVINS
& CARROLL MULTZ

BARKING
FROG

LIVONIA, MICHIGAN

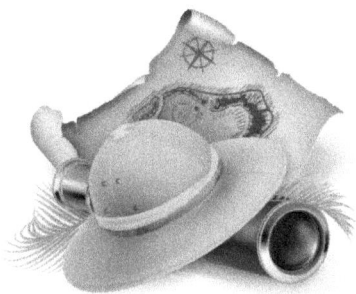

PROLOGUE

Our newly formed club, the *Are You One Toos (R*U*1*2s* for short), has close to two dozen members ranging in age from five to twelve years old. All the members live in and around our neighborhood and each was instrumental in converting an old apple shed into a fitting clubhouse.

Homer Pearson, who sometimes went by his middle name Lloyd, Rhymin' Sally's father, gave us permission to use the shed as a clubhouse after Sally, a precocious five-year old, was threatened by a band of thugs. It's been almost a year since Sally was rescued from the lawless group, who as it turned out, had been cruising our neighborhood looking for something to steal or destroy. They descended on the apple stand on the edge of the apple orchard manned by Sally and her mother like a swarm of bees. Apparently, the thugs had staked out the stand as a target, and when Sally was left alone while her mother sought to replenish the apple supply, they struck.

The thugs would have made off with the cash drawer had it not been for a group of neighborhood youngsters returning from a school function and who just happened to be passing by the stand. Seeing what was happening, they immediately sprung to Sally's aid. I am proud to say I was part of that group. We struggled with the intruders before the thugs were frightened away by Sally's mother who, after seeing what was taking place, used her cell phone to summon Sally's father. When Sally's father arrived and was told about the heroic actions, he praised us and a bond was forged between the Pearsons and our neighborhood group.

"What can we do to repay you?" Homer Pearson had asked.

"Aw, it was nothing. We don't need to be repaid," either Genius or I replied.

However, when Sally's father was persistent and insisted he be given the opportunity to repay us, I pointed to an abandoned apple storage shed that had stood vacant for a number of years in the middle of the Pearsons' apple orchard and said, "We are in the process of forming a club to occupy us for the summer and could use your apple shed as a clubhouse."

"It's yours," Sally's father replied without hesitation. "I'll meet you at the apple shed tomorrow at noon. We, that is the Pearson three, will have lunch waiting for you and your friends and we'll explore what needs to be done to fashion that dilapidated old shed into a suitable clubhouse."

"Yippee!" we all shouted.

The next day, with some of our fellow classmates, neighbors and friends, we descended upon the orchard. There were at least twenty-four in number. And as promised, the Pearsons had lunch waiting. After everyone had settled in, Sally asked each of us, one-by-one, if we were one of the heroes who had rescued her the day before.

"Are you one too?" I remember her asking. And so it came to pass that the name of our newly formed club was conceived. From that point forward, we would be known as the *Are You One Toos (R*U*1*2s)*. All those present, including Sally, became the coveted charter members.

With the help of Homer Pearson, we furnished the clubhouse with empty packing crates and other odds and ends we gathered from our families. Our mothers took turns providing sandwiches, drinks and snacks. It is cool inside the converted apple storage shed because the apple trees outside provide shade and a persistent breeze wafts through the open door and windows as if on cue.

The clubhouse was soon jammed with an assortment of games and books. During these summer months, Genius and I took turns reading to our fellow *R*U*1*2s*. Our eighth-grade teacher to be had challenged us to do something over the summer to promote education in our respective neighborhoods. At first, we did this to satisfy the homework assignment but it was not long before we discovered it was not only educational but fun as well.

Everyone looks forward to our reading sessions. The reading sessions have not only become a hobby, but an obsession, and needless to say, our parents are delighted that we are not whittling away our time or getting into mischief.

It was not long before we outgrew the apple storage shed and moved our clubhouse to the larger bunkhouse at the other end of the orchard.

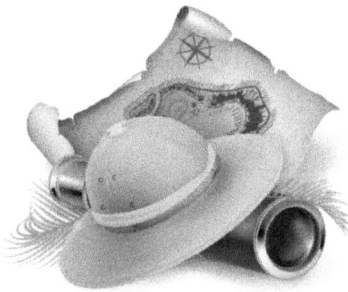

CHAPTER ONE

THE TRUNK

My name is Shacoo Bandaris. I'm twelve years old and live with my parents in Jefferson City, Iowa. I will be in the eighth grade at Thomas Jefferson Middle School when school starts this fall. My mother's name is Katrina, but my father and her friends call her Katie; my father's name is Carlo. He is a biologist and employed as a lab technician for Chemical Technology Resources, Inc. here in Jefferson City.

My grandparents, Andria and Tomaso Bandaris, maintain the family's ancestral home located just a few miles from where I live with my parents. I've proven to Mom and Dad that I'm responsible, so when I turned twelve they gave their consent for me to ride my bike to my grandparents for an occasional visit. Although I know I'm always welcome, I still phone ahead for permission to come see them.

"Hello," Grandma Andria answers when I call today.

"Grandma, it's Shacoo." Grandma's hearing is not too good so I talk louder than usual and identify myself as I'm not sure she recognizes my voice.

"Shacoo, how nice to hear from you."

"Thank you, Grandma. If you and Grandpa aren't busy, would it be okay if I came by for a visit this afternoon?"

"Never too busy for you, Shacoo. We'd love to see you."

"Oh, good! I still have a couple of things to do before I leave, so it'll be about one-thirty before I get there."

"We'll be expecting you. Grandpa will be pleased when I tell him you're coming. Be safe."

✳

I'M EXCITED FOR THE visit with my grandparents so I hurry to finish my chores. When I take out the trash, I spot five-year-old Rhymin' Sally coming up the street in my direction. As she approaches, she says,

> *Hi, Shacoo. Mommy said I could come see you.*
> *If you're not busy today, would you like to play?*

Sally is the youngest member of the *R*U*1*2s*. She earned the name Rhymin' Sally because, from the time she started talking, she spoke in rhymes. And even today, it's still a mystery as to why she started talking in rhymes. I've babysat her many times and I like to think of her as the little sister I never had.

"Hi, Sally," I say. "I do have plans for today. I'm going to visit my grandparents this afternoon."

> *Oh, I see.*
> *Tell them hello for me.*

"I will for sure," and when I notice a dejected look cross Sally's face, I add, "Maybe we can do something later this week." At my suggestion, Sally perks up.

> *Okay.*

Hope you have a nice day.

I stand and watch Sally turn toward home. I feel bad because I can't play with her today. My fear is that if she gets bored, her unique imagination will run away with her—again. I suddenly cringe when I remember that, on a couple of occasions, Sally materialized her favorite characters from the pages of two of her storybooks—first, Snow White, and later Little Red Riding Hood. These two events created challenging situations for the *R*U*1*2s*. Not only did she materialize Snow White, but also Snow's supporting cast of characters. We had seven little men running around the clubhouse looking for their mine so they could go to work. When Little Red Riding Hood emerged from the storybook, so did The Big Bad Wolf. We lived in fear thinking that he was roaming around the orchard looking for his next meal. Those were chaotic times and I flinch when I recount the harrowing events.

I watch Sally slowly walk back toward her home and seeking assurance, I call after her, "You gonna be okay? And you know what I mean."

Sally turns back and with a sheepish look on her face, says,

You needn't worry about that Shacoo,
I learned my lesson and know what not to do.
Besides, you took away my magic wand,
So I can't bring anyone here from beyond.
And I wouldn't, even if I could,
'Cause I promised you I'd be good.

I breathe a sigh of relief knowing that Sally can acknowledge her mistakes and apparently learn from them.

"I have something very important to do, but I'll call you later in the week. We'll make your favorite chocolate chip cookies."

Oh boy!

Can I bring Baby Doll One and Baby Doll Two?

You know that they like to make cookies, too.

"Of course you can! The more the merrier." *Oops, wish I hadn't said that! She might take me seriously and invite Hansel and Gretel.*

✳

WHEN I ARRIVE AT my grandparents' home, as is my custom, I walk my bike around the garage side of the house and enter through the backdoor. I find Grandma in the kitchen clearing the lunch dishes. After we exchange hugs, she points to the side of the house.

"Your Grandpa is on the porch waiting for you," she says. "Go on out now, I'll join you later—with some lemonade." Grandma points to a glass pitcher on the counter top. Slices of lemon float around it in a swirl and it looks very inviting.

"Umm, looks good," I say. "Can I do anything to help you, Grandma?"

"Thank you, honey. I'm just 'bout finished, I'll be right behind you," she says. "Go on, now. Don't keep your grandpa waitin'."

I head for the other side of the house, and as soon as I open the squeaky screen door, Grandpa turns and smiles. "Shacoo, get on over here," he says, and pats the space beside him.

"Hi, Grandpa," I say, as I eagerly join him on the old wooden porch swing. It squeaks, too, as we rock back and forth. "It's nice and cool here on the veranda."

"Yep, this is one of my favorite places—except for the uninvited guests." He swats at a pesky fly that keeps buzzing around his face.

✳

ONE OF THE REASONS I look forward to these visits besides loving my grandparents, of course, is that Grandpa is the family historian and he always has a tale to tell. I find Grandpa Tomaso's stories interesting as well as educational and today is no different.

The July afternoon heat is bearing down on us as we gently rock the porch swing back and forth sipping the lemonade provided by Grandma Andria. I sit transfixed, listening intently as Grandpa transports me back in time to the eighteen hundreds. He's telling a story of how his grandparents, that would be my Great-Great-Grandparents Giovanni and Maria Bandaris, immigrated to America.

"Wish you could've known them," He says, as he gazes off into the distance.

"Me, too," I reply.

Grandpa scratches his chin in what looks like thoughtful reflection. He then says, "We have a trunk in the attic that belonged to my father; that would be your Great Grandpa Lorenzo. If I remember right, there are some tintypes and other memorabilia stored in that old relic, some of which belonged to your Great-Great Grandparents, Giovanni and Maria."

One of Grandpa's favorite teases is burying unfamiliar words in his sentences. He chooses ones he feels sure I won't recognize. It's a game we play and I must admit his ploy has been beneficial in increasing my vocabulary. When I hear the word tintype, I'm on full alert. I instantly know that tintype is the word for the day,

I take the bait, "What's a tintype?" I ask.

A wide grin spreads across Grandpa's face. He says, "Tintypes are the forerunners of photographs. They're called tintypes because, in the late eighteen and early nineteen hundreds, photographs were made by creating images on sheets of thin metal."

"Oh, my!" I exclaim. As excitement ripples through me, I ask, "May I see them?"

"Of course," he replies, "hopefully they haven't faded beyond recognition."

I'm filled with anticipation at the prospect of seeing photographs of my ancestors. I push on, "Can we get them now?"

Grandpa slowly leans forward as if to stand and I notice a grimace cross his face. Then rubbing his left hip with his fingertips, he sinks back onto the swing and says, "I'm sorry, honey, but my hip has been acting up and I'm not able to climb those steep stairs to the attic, at least not for a while. Maybe some other time."

"Oh," I sigh.

He must have detected the disappointment in my voice because he says, "Of course, Shacoo, if you're not afraid of mice, spiders and other miscellaneous attic creatures, you can go on up there on your own and look through my father's old trunk."

"I'm not afraid!" I squeal and jump up and give him a big hug.

✳

AS SOON AS I reach the top of the steep flight of stairs leading to the attic, chills run up and down my spine. Turning, I look down the stairs and mentally plan an escape route—just in case I need one. I'm experiencing the same uneasiness I felt when Genius, Tank and I first entered the foreboding Bradbury Mansion last summer. Genius and Tank are my best friends, fellow classmates and R*U*1*2 members. Although we did encounter a spirit, our experience with a ghost named Lucinda Bradbury was far from frightening. Now that I know for certain that ghosts, or spirits, exist, I'm no longer afraid of them or the thought of them. However, I also realize that not all spirits are as friendly as Lucinda.

Standing there before the attic door, I feel foolish because of my apprehension and my tendency to let my imagination run away with me. However, my desire to explore past family records and see photographs of my ancestors overrules my anxiety and I brush aside my uneasiness.

I turn the doorknob and when I give the door a gentle push, the rusty hinges creak as the door slowly opens. Instantly, a musty odor from the hot, stuffy, unventilated upper story penetrates my nostrils and I vigorously wave my hands in front of my face in an attempt to dispel the smell. When I take a few steps into the dimly lit chamber, I immediately become entangled in a curtain of creepy cobwebs that cling to my face and arms.

"Yipes!" I cry as I swipe at the cobwebs, brushing the icky film from my skin and clothing.

That eerie Bradbury Mansion feeling returns and I'm beginning to doubt my bravado. Just as I'm on the verge of fleeing, I imagine Genius chastising me. *Since when do you back down from a challenge? Are you going to be a sissy and let a few cobwebs frighten you away?* The thought of being taunted by Genius strengthens my resolve and I proceed further into the interior of the mysterious room.

My eyes soon grow accustomed to the gloom and I slowly walk through the maze of antique furniture and odds and ends that have accumulated over the years, and probably even over the century. My movements stir up the layers of dust that cover every surface. I watch clouds of the fine powder dance in the slivers of sunlight that pierce the slats of the broken shutter that clings by a single hinge to the outside of the attic window. Each time I move, I stir up more dust and my eyes begin to itch and my throat feels dry. I look back at the door, my escape route, and suppress the urge to run. I've come this far, so I ignore my better judgment which is nagging me to flee, and continue to explore my surroundings.

Wandering about the stuffy archive, I start to appreciate the treasure trove of stored items that beckons to me. Each of the discards from the past could probably tell a fascinating story of its own. I'm now aided by a hanging light fixture which I activate by just tightening the bulb. I examine what appears to be a miniature antique china cabinet filled with crystal glassware and fine bone china. The china has sprays of pastel flowers dancing around its borders. When I open the drawer to the china cabinet, I discover a stack of delicate linens with elaborate patterns embroidered at the corners and on the edges. *Were these linens used only on special holidays or to entertain important guests such as senators, governors or heroes of the day?*

I slowly move past the china cabinet and find a small steamer trunk that stands partially open against the wall. It's overflowing with several colorful intricate-patterned handmade bed quilts. I'm awed at the sight of such craftsmanship and beauty. *Which of my ancestors had the patience to piece these lovely quilts together?*

Moving further into the attic, I come upon what must have been a child's play area. I slowly walk through and as if in a nineteenth century dream, I visualize children playing with the toys that are scattered about. I activate another hanging light bulb. I'm mesmerized by the array of toys and carefully examine each of the objects piece-by-piece. There is a sweet doll-size wicker baby carriage that is missing a wheel; a weather-beaten wooden rocking horse that looks as though it once was painted to resemble the horses on a merry-go-round; a matted, honey colored fuzzy shop worn teddy bear missing an ear; a set of different sized wooden building blocks housed in a small rolling cart with a string attached for pulling the blocks from place to place; a small round drum with patriotic symbols painted on the sides; assorted jacks and marbles jumbled together in a small box; and a porcelain baby doll resting on an array of doll clothes nestled in an old shoe box. The doll's clothes look like what I imagine little girls wore a hundred years ago. I marvel that the toys of yesteryear are similar to those of today's youth. I can almost hear the laughter of the turn-of-the-century children as they frolicked here in their attic sanctuary. I lift the doll and cradle her in my arms; the paint is almost worn off her cherub-like face, but I can still detect a slight smile on her pursed lips. *What lucky girl loved you all those many years ago?*

When I replace the doll, I look up and my attention is drawn to a tattered old trunk on the other side of the room. Could this be the object I've been seeking? The thought of what I might discover when I lift the lid intrigues me. I sense an exciting adventure is waiting for me on the other side of the dust-covered lid.

I'm so focused on my target that I'm startled when Grandpa calls up to me, "How ya doin' up there?"

Grandpa's loud voice jerks me into the present. I call back, "Just found the trunk. Haven't opened it yet."

"Take your time," he grunts. "Grandma went to the grocery store and I think I'm going to lay down for a bit."

"Okay, thank you, Grandpa."

✳

TURNING MY ATTENTION BACK to the trunk, I determine that I need something to wipe the lid. It's much too dusty to open and I don't want the dust to filter into the trunk when I lift the cover. I look around and find a rag nearby and use it to dust the top of the trunk.

When I remove the layer of dust, I notice a tarnished brass nameplate riveted to the lid. It is eloquently engraved with great-great grandfather's name, Giovanni Bandaris. My heart skips a beat and my hands tremble as I grasp the leather handle attached to the front of the lid and ease it upward.

After years of lying dormant, the lid groans as I open it. Perhaps it's protesting my interrupting its peaceful retirement here in the attic. The first thing I see inside the trunk is a shallow tray that spans the width and breadth of the trunk. It contains a Bible and an assortment of other books of the day. I recognize the titles, some of which are still popular; Pride and Prejudice, Jane Eyre, Wuthering Heights, Little Women and more. I also find a copy of a nineteenth century almanac along with a pair of reading glasses resting in a carved wooden case. I don't disturb the books because they are fragile and yellowed with age. I realize they could be valuable and easily damaged by carelessly handling them. However, before I remove the tray and set it aside, I carefully examine the Bible. I know special events are usually recorded in family Bibles and I'm elated when I find the special events page has been filled in. Listed in chronological order are births, baptisms, weddings and deaths. I study the entries and recognize most of the names of relatives woven into grandpa's stories.

I replace the Bible and remove the top tray and set it aside. Under it, I find that the next layer contains clothing which is wrapped in heavy brown paper, probably for protection. I lift out the first article and carefully unwrap it. When I see the contents, I gasp with delight. I'm gazing at what must have been Great-Great Grandma Maria's wedding gown. Although dingy from lying in the trunk for so many years, it's still beautiful. I gently pick it up and as the long silk skirt gracefully unfolds, rays of light dance across the ribbon rosettes and seed pearls that embellish the bodice. I caress the garment before I lovingly rewrap it and lay it aside. *If I ever get married, I want to be married in this gown.* The only other article of clothing in the trunk is what looks like a military uniform. The insignia on the epaulettes are foreign to me and no doubt are Italian. *Is this what Great-Great Grandpa Giovanni wore when he married Maria?*

I set aside the clothing and when I do, I discover a tin box and a journal resting at the bottom of the trunk. I examine the box first in the hopes that it contains the tintypes Grandpa Tomaso had mentioned. I'm not disappointed. There are five tintype pictures in the box. One is a wedding pose of a couple dressed in the garments I found in the trunk. I'm guessing the man and woman are my great-great grandparents. The other tintypes are images of people I do not recognize; some of the men are wearing the same type of military uniform as the man in the wedding picture. *I'll take the tintypes downstairs with me. Maybe Grandpa Tomaso can identify some of those who are pictured.*

Last but not least, I pick up the journal. Something inside of me whispers exciting adventures lie within its pages and are just waiting to be released. Before I open the journal, I repack everything, except the box containing the tintypes. I shut the lid, satisfied the precious contents are once again secure inside the confines of the trunk. I take the journal and move to a spot where the light is better. Sitting cross-legged on the floor, I begin my journey into the past.

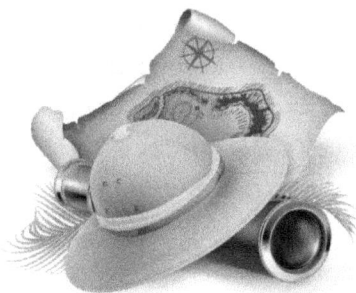

CHAPTER TWO

THE JOURNAL

The leather cover of the journal is tooled with fancy swirls around the border and tied with a thin strip of leather that wraps around it twice. Both the cover and tie are darkened from having been handled many times. I reverently open the journal and when I do I find that it is written in fine script. The memoir begins the day my great-great-grandparents arrived in America. I immediately conclude the entries were made by my Great-Great-Grandpa Giovanni. This delights me. I feel as though he is speaking to me personally as I begin reading the journal.

When I'm partway through the chronicle, I discover that some of the entries have numbers written in the margin adjacent to them. Even though these entries are no different than the rest, it's obvious they have some significance. The entries with numbers in the margins read:

July 3, 1876

My name is Giovanni Bandaris. I am immigrant coming to America from Italy. I arrive with my new bride, Maria. We marry one month ago. What a wonderful way to start new life in new country. We fold hands and give thanks to God.   5/2-3 3

July 4, 1876

As soon as we come ashore, we are caught up in big celebration with fireworks and marching bands. We later learn that America is celebrating anniversary of her 100 year of becoming an independent nation. We're proud to be here.   4/4 4

August 16, 1876

New York much too big. We now join other immigrants and go to Jefferson City. Reminds us of home in Italy where sun shines all day. I work for farmer and he let us use small house.   3/5-6 2

September 12, 1876

Life is good in new country. Many foreign people where we live. They make me mayor of Jefferson City. Maria very proud. We are given different home, much nicer, but Maria complain too many steps.   5/2 5

October 31, 1876

We celebrate strange American holiday. Many children and others play make believe and wear costumes. Town people tell me I must have party and make Maria and me wear funny clothes. Our faces are hidden by masks. We like and have much fun.

5/4 6

November 30, 1876

Today is American Thanksgiving holiday. Maria and me treasure our new homeland and much to be thankful for.

2/3 7

December 24, 1876

After fire burn house, Maria see nice house she wants. I have money I bring from Italy so I buy for Christmas. It is Victorian and many rooms. We very happy when we move. Good view of Sleeping Giant Mesa in distance.

5/2-3 1

April 16, 1878

It's spring and Maria likes to walk on mesa. I worry when she gone too long. There are many hazards on mesa and I fear she will become lost in cave or get bit by snake.

4/2 8

May 3, 1878

*Today Maria is gone long time. I go look for her.
I climb Sleeping Giant Mesa and look all around.
I find her sitting on high rock shelf in noon day
sun. She not hurt.*

3/6-8 9

3/10-11 10

4/1 10

I'm completely baffled as I try to determine what the numbers in the margins represent. If Grandpa doesn't know, I'll ask if I can take the journal for a few days and run it by Genius. Genius has an analytical mind and is good at solving puzzles.

I close the journal, and getting ready to leave, I stand and brush the dust off my jeans. Although I was apprehensive when I first entered the attic chamber, I'm now actually sorry that I must go. I do a 360 and look around to make sure I'm leaving the attic the way I found it and as I walk out, I unscrew the two light bulbs on my way back to the staircase. With the metal box containing the tintypes and the journal, I reluctantly leave the attic.

✳

GRANDPA SEEMS TO BE refreshed from his nap and I find him sitting on the porch swing enjoying the coolness of the late afternoon. "Hey, Shacoo. Come sit by me," he says. Then apparently noticing the objects I'm carrying, he asks, "What ya got there?"

I sit down beside him and secure the objects next to me on the swing. I first take the metal box containing the tintypes. "I found this in one of the trunks," I say and open the box and hand it to him. The wedding tintype is on the top.

"That's it!" he exclaims. "That was taken at the wedding of Grandpa and Grandma Bandaris." He picks up the picture and holding it close to his face, he examines it. He glances at me and I detect tears in his eyes. Looking down, he hurriedly pulls his handkerchief from his hip pocket and snorting into it, says, "Darn allergies."

Not wanting to embarrass him, I act as though I don't notice his emotional reaction and say, "Are all of the others photographs of relatives?" and point to the remaining four in the box.

Grandpa takes the tintypes from the box and studies them one by one. He finally shakes his head and says, "I don't recognize any of them. I'll ask your grandma when she returns from the grocery." Then looking past me at the journal, he asks, "What else did ya find?"

I pick up the leather-bound journal and when I hand it to him, his face lights up. "I'd forgotten about this." He opens it and as he leafs through the pages, he says, "This is a personal history of your great-great grandparents." And again I notice a return of the "darn allergies."

"Grandpa," I say, "As I went through the journal, I noticed some funny markings in the margins of some of the entries."

He nods his head. "Yes, I remember seeing those many years ago myself when I read the journal."

"Do you know what they mean?" I ask.

"Nope, not a clue," he says shaking his head. "Grandma and I spent many hours trying to figure out what the numbers meant. In the end we decided that whatever the answer was, Grandpa Giovanni took it with him to his grave."

I'd been thinking about the numbers and decided if Grandpa didn't know what they meant, I'd ask if I could have Genius take a look at them. Grandpa seems to be distracted so I decide it's now or never. I say, "You remember my friend, Genius? I think you've met him on several occasions."

"Why, yes. Nice young fellow. What about him?"

"Well, Grandpa, he's smart—that's why we call him Genius. He played a big part in helping the police solve the cases of the cat burglar that plagued Jefferson City and the bank robber that kidnapped me."

"Yes, I do remember that."

"If you'd allow me to take the journal for a little while, I'll see if Genius can solve the mystery."

Grandpa looks unsure for a few moments as he fingers the journal. "You know, Shacoo, you've proven yourself to be responsible and trustworthy. I'm sure Genius is also. I'm willing to let you take it and if you figure out it's a treasure map, you can keep the booty." Then Grandpa laughs, "I'm too old to go treasure hunting anyway. Besides, I have everything I'll ever need."

I'm elated that I get to take the journal and Grandpa's faith in me means even more. I trace an X over my heart, and say, "I know the journal is priceless and I promise I won't let anything happen to it. You have my word."

"If I can't trust you, then who can I trust?" He smiles and adds, "Your grandma's the one who suggested the journal might contain a hidden message as to where a treasure might be buried. Who knows? She might be right."

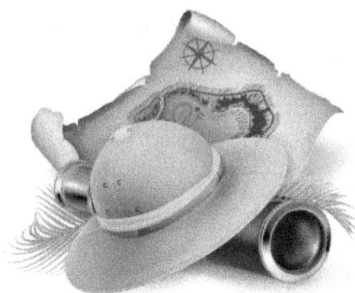

CHAPTER THREE
THE MYSTERY

Returning to the rear of my grandparents' home, I retrieve my bike and walk it around to the front of the house. Grandpa meets me at the front and hands me the journal. I carefully wrap it in a light jacket I carry with me in my saddlebag to make sure it is not damaged. After easing the journal into the saddlebag, I buckle the straps and mount my bike. When I'm ready to leave, I say, "Don't worry about the journal, Grandpa, I'll guard it with my life."

"Whoa now! Let's not go that far. There's nothing worth unnecessarily risking your life. All I expect is that you respect it for its historical value and the promise it contains."

"Absolutely! You know I will."

"Yes, I do know you will. And good luck in deciphering the code."

✸

I'M FULL OF EXCITEMENT as I peddle toward home as fast as I can. As soon as I get home, I call Genius.

"Hello."

"Genius, I need to see you right away."

"Is something wrong?" Genius asks. I detect concern in his voice.

"Oh no! Sorry, didn't mean to alarm you. I just came from visiting my grandparents and I have something I want to share with you."

"You sound pretty excited. Do you want me to come over?"

"If it's all the same to you, I'd rather meet at the clubhouse. No one will be there this late in the day. I want to keep what I have to share a secret, for a while anyway."

"Now I'm really curious. How soon can you get there?" he asks.

"I'm on my way as soon as we hang up."

✳

I ARRIVE FIRST AND sit down on the porch steps as I wait for Genius. When I see him peddling down the lane, I stand and wave to him. He waves back and when he arrives he comes to a screeching halt in front of the clubhouse.

"Now what's this all about?" he breathlessly asks.

I beckon to him with my hand, "Come in, this is a show and tell situation."

Genius parks his bike and bounds up the steps. Once we're inside the clubhouse I motion for him to take a seat at the table next to me. When we're situated, I produce the journal.

"What is that?" he asks.

I painstakingly go through the events of the day. When I get to the part about how I found the journal and the mystery that it holds. I open it to one of the entries with the numbers in the margin. I slide it over in front of Genius and say, "See, this is what I'm talking about."

"I see," he says, "very perplexing." After closely examining the entry, he asks, "How many entries are there with numbers in the margins?"

"Nine. However, the last one has two sets of numbers recorded in the margin."

"Okay. Show me that one."

I turn to the page with the entry containing the two sets of numbers and point to them. "Here," I say.

"Uh-huh. Very, very interesting."

Genius frowns. I recognize this expression. It means he is now oblivious to the world around him and absorbed in solving the problem at hand. After studying the journal at length, he asks, "Did your grandpa have any idea about what the entries could mean?"

"No, none. He said that he and grandma studied the entries on several occasions. They finally gave up as nothing occurred to them except that they contained some type of code."

I know Genius well enough to recognize when he's baffled. He softly says, "A code to what? A buried treasure?"

"Quick thinking, Sherlock," I reply. "How we break the code is the issue of the day. Think you can do it?"

I sense he is no longer listening to me and I watch as he rubs his palms together. He's onto something.

"I need a pencil and pad," he murmurs, not looking up from the journal. I oblige by getting the requested items from the drawer in the kitchen cabinet.

When I hand them to Genius, he nods. He painstakingly designs a grid on the pad. I watch as he draws four vertical lines the length of the pad and then makes ten horizontal rows the width of the pad. At the top of each section, he pencils in headings: Date, Single #s, Multiple #s, and Words.

After studying the grid for several long minutes, Genius says, "I don't think the date of entry has any significance in solving the puzzle. I believe the single numbers at the end of the entries are the order in which the clues are to be put together."

He pencils in the single numbers, one through ten on the horizontal lines beneath the heading Single #s.

"Now if I could just figure out what the multiple numbers represent..." he says.

I sit in silence as I watch Genius continue to examine the journal.

"If you'll notice, the entries contain four or more lines in the narration except for number seven. Number seven has only three lines and the multiple numbers adjacent to number seven are 2/3. So by taking line 2 and the third word of the sentence, we come up with *treasure*."

I nod, as I mentally follow what he is explaining.

Genius writes the word *treasure* in slot number 7 on the grid. When I realize that he may be close to solving the mystery, my heart starts pounding and my hands shake. I marvel at Genius' intellect as I watch him continue to work through the puzzle.

"Okay, starting with the first journal entry, single number 3, and by taking line number 5 and the 1st and 2nd words, we get *folded hands*. Shacoo, write *folded hands* in slot three on the grid. Now, the next entry in the journal points to line 4 and the 4th word or number which gives us...*100*." Genius points to me, "Write *100* on line four on the grid."

As Genius plows through the entries I write the words he gives me on the grid. "Write *sun shines* in the number two slot; *steps* in the number five slot; *hidden* in the number 6 slot; *Sleeping Giant* in the number one slot; *cave* in the number eight slot;

high rock shelf in the number 9 slot; and *noon day sun* in the number ten slot."

When we're finished, the grid looks like this:

Date	Single #s	Multiple #s	Words
12/24/1876	1	5/2-3	Sleeping Giant
08/16/1876	2	3/5-6	sun shines
07/03/1876	3	5/1-2	folded hands
07/04/1876	4	4/4	100
09/12/1876	5	5/1	steps
10/31/1876	6	5/4	hidden
11/30/1876	7	2/3	treasure
04/16/1877	8	4/2	cave
05/03/1877	9	3/6-8	high rock shelf
05/03/1877	10	3/10-11&4/1	noon day sun

Genius examines the grid then slides the pad over in front of me and says, "Okay, Shacoo, please read the words from top to bottom."

I trace my finger down the grid as I read the entries one-by-one. "Sleeping Giant, sun shines, folded hands, 100, steps, hidden, treasure, cave, high rock shelf, noon day sun." When I finish, I look up at Genius and ask, "Does this mean that there is hidden treasure on a high rock shelf in a cave that can be found on Sleeping Giant Mesa by going 100 steps in the noon day sun that shines through the giant's folded hands?"

"Precisely, Dr. Watson, precisely. By Jove, I think we've got it!"

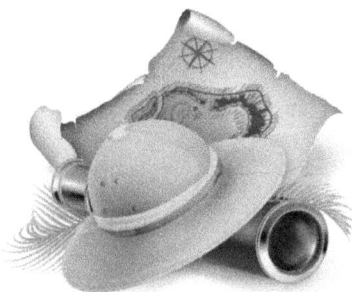

CHAPTER FOUR

THE SEARCH

'm bubbling over with excitement and can't wait to test Genius' theory. However, I suspect that if I tell my grandparents that we think we have broken the code and that it is indeed a treasure map, they would consider it too dangerous for us to explore and forbid us from searching for the hidden treasure. *But if we don't mention it, that might be considered deceptive.*

✳

THE NEXT MORNING, I excitedly place a call to Genius.

"Hello."

"Genius," I say, "I have a plan."

"Okay," then after a pause, he asks, "What are you talking about?"

"Oh, sorry, I'm getting ahead of myself. I'm referring to searching for the treasure."

"Yes, it is intriguing and I've been thinking about that as well. What's your plan?"

JUDITH BLEVINS & CARROLL MULTZ

"Well, you know how grownups can be. I'm afraid if I tell my grandparents about what we suspect the code means they might not let us explore Sleeping Giant Mesa, especially looking for treasure."

"You're probably right, but…"

"Just hold on, here's my plan. Our parents have allowed us to ride our bikes up to Sleeping Giant Mesa on several occasions. If we don't say anything about hunting for a treasure, we wouldn't be disobeying orders."

"WE?"

"Well, of course we. You, me and Tank. If you refuse, I'll do it alone. And besides, Grandpa said if it was a treasure map, and I found the treasure, I could keep it."

"Well—"

"Well what? I've never known you to back off an adventure and especially one that could be the adventure of a lifetime." I sense Genius is weakening so I push on, "The mesa is really not that far and if we get an early start…"

"Okay! You talked me into it! I thought about it all night, and seriously, I can't wait to get started either. I'll call Tank and have him meet us at my house. Tank had called me earlier and said he was bored. He said he is looking for something to do."

"That's more like the Genius I know." Then after a pause I say, "I have a flashlight. Can you think of anything else we may need?"

"Hmm, I'll bring my Boy Scout first aid kit and some rope. You may want to throw in some PBJ sandwiches and I'll bring water."

"I'll be there as soon as I clear it with mom. She knew I was not eager to go shopping with her today."

"I'll get a hold of Tank and we'll meet you at the clubhouse."

✳

IN LESS THAN FORTY-FIVE minutes, the three of us are peddling up the steep slope, grinding our way to the top of Sleeping Giant Mesa. This time I don't even notice how difficult the trek is, probably because of the excited state I'm in. Thinking of the possibility of discovering a hidden treasure is the only thing on my mind.

"Hey, can we rest for a minute?" Tank pleads as he pulls to a stop.

Genius stops behind him and stands straddling his bike. "Sure," he says and then hands Tank a bottle of water.

I stop and walk my bike to where the boys are resting. "This July heat is bad even this early in the day," I say, wiping my brow with my forearm. I gratefully take the bottle of water Genius offers me.

"And it's going to get worse," Genius says. "Come on, break is over. Let's get going."

I look up to the top of the mesa and calculate that we're almost half way there. "How long do you think it'll take to reach the summit?" I ask, as we start out again.

"Hard to say," Genius replies and looks at his watch. "It's taken an hour just to get this far."

"But that was mainly on flat terrain." Tank says. "Surely we can make it to the top in less time than an hour."

"True!" Genius remarks. "However, it's uphill the rest of the way—which will take considerably longer than riding on a flat surface."

"Okay, okay!" I say. "Let's save our energy for the ride, not the chide."

Tank looks at me over his shoulder and smirks, "You got Sally in your saddlebag?"

"Very funny!" I say. He's no doubt referring to the rhyming of the words ride and chide. "Sally doesn't have a monopoly," I add and we all laugh.

✳

APPROXIMATELY FORTY MINUTES LATER, we reach the summit of Sleeping Giant Mesa. Exhausted, we secure our bikes and flop down in the shade of a stand of trees to rest a few minutes before we ditch the bikes and start the even steeper climb on foot. We survey the stone formation that resembles a sleeping giant. Because of the amount of hikers to and from the popular tourist attraction, there is a worn pathway up to nature's version of a sleeping giant. Standing at the feet of the formation, we gaze at its mass, marveling at how perfectly it resembles that of a reclining giant with his hands folded on his chest.

"How are we going to get to the designated area before the noonday sun?" Tank asks as he checks his watch. "We probably have less than twenty minutes."

"Oh ye of little faith," Genius replies. "I researched the mesa last night and found that there are crude stairs carved on the other side of the formation. They go straight up to the folded hands."

"Duh! Then why are we just standing here?" I say. And the three of us race around to the other side of the formation.

The stairs, indentations dug out in the dirt slope, are irregular and narrow. Genius takes the lead and Tank and I very carefully follow him. Because of the rough terrain and unstable footing, it takes us almost fifteen minutes to get to the top. When Tank and I finally catch up to Genius, he's already crawling through the giant's folded hands into the space the opening has created on the giant's torso.

"Hurry up," he shouts. "The sun is almost in position."

Tank and I crawl on our hands and knees to where Genius is stationed waiting for the noonday sun. As the three of us cluster together, the sun gradually creeps upward. We watch in amazement as a wedge of sunlight seeps through the folded hands and spreads the length of the giant's body.

Wasting no time, Genius shouts, "Come on, follow me," and he moves to the beginning of the wedge of sunlight and starts walking, counting off paces as he goes. Tank and I follow in his footsteps.

"…ninety-eight, ninety-nine, one hundred," Genius says as he stops and holds up a hand signaling for us to stay where we are. Tank and I stop, frozen in our tracks. We're surprised when suddenly, the wedge of sunlight vanishes. It disappears just as quickly as it appeared.

We watch as Genius slowly turns in all directions surveying the area. "I don't see anything that looks like a cave," he says and I detect disappointment in his voice.

He sits down and crossing his arms on his bent knees, rests his head on his arms. We join him and we sit in silence for a few long minutes. In his frustration, Genius picks up a large stone and hurls it into the brush in front of us. We're all surprised when the rock rebounds off of what appears to be a solid surface behind the overgrown shrubbery.

Genius jumps up, "That's it! That must be where the cave is hidden," he says and rushes to the spot where the stone hit. By the time Tank and I catch up, he is vigorously ripping the shrubbery away from the site, exposing a rock surface with an opening leading into a dark cavern.

"Shacoo, hand me your flashlight," he orders. His voice is laced with excitement. I pull my flashlight from my back pack and hand it to Genius. "Thank you," he says and shines the light into the cave slowly moving it around on the walls. We watch huddled together at the entrance. Genius suddenly stops and moves the light back a few feet.

JUDITH BLEVINS & CARROLL MULTZ

"Look there," he says, as he shines the light over a small area. "I think I saw a rock shelf…" He then moves the light forward a few inches, "YES! I did see a shelf. Look, there it is," and he points the beam of the flashlight upward.

Tank and I look up to where the light is shining and see a rock ledge protruding from the wall about three or four feet from the ceiling on the far end of the cave.

"Genius, do you think…" I say.

"One way to find out," he says and he starts forward into the cave.

"NO! WAIT!" Tank shouts, stopping Genius in his tracks.

"What? Why?" Genius replies.

"Well, I think we should proceed more cautiously. I've seen movies where the prize is protected by a series of booby traps. How can we be sure the cave isn't loaded with pitfalls?"

Genius steps back and looks at Tank. The expression on his face is pure terror. "You're right! I wasn't thinking." He then shines the light on the dirt floor of the cave and carefully maneuvers it around. "Anything look suspicious?" he asks.

"That's the point," Tank answers. "A booby trap wouldn't be obvious to the naked eye."

"Right again," Genius whispers.

"What do we do now?" I ask.

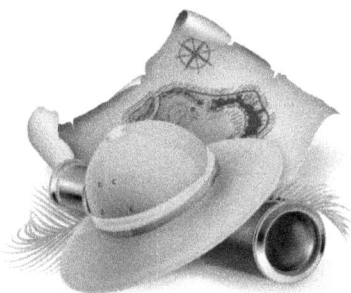

CHAPTER FIVE
PERILOUS JOURNEY

"Okay, Tank," Genius says, "how do your movie heroes get past the traps?"

Tank looks thoughtful for a few moments and then says, "Sometimes they don't. They just deal with the traps as they're sprung on them."

"Not too reassuring," I say.

"Hey, don't blame me," Tank replies. "I'm just trying to avoid anyone getting hurt or killed or worse."

"Or worse? What could be worse?" I ask.

"Calm down, you two," Genius says. "We need to approach this situation logically."

Tank and I look at each other. "What do you have in mind?" I ask Genius, not sure this situation can be approached logically.

"Stay here, I'll be right back," Genius says and heads toward where we left our bicycles. When he returns, he's carrying a coil of rope that is thin and resembles that used for clotheslines.

"This is what we're going to do," he says, as he uncoils the rope on the ground before us. Tank and I watch as he slides one end of the rope through a small loop he fashioned at the other end. He then steps through the rope bringing the loop up and securing it around his waist.

Handing the free end of the rope to Tank, Genius says, "Wrap this around that tree over there and hang onto it, keeping it taut. I'm going to go into the cave and see if I can locate the rock ledge. If I jerk on the rope twice, pull me out. Otherwise, just stand by…"

Wide eyed with fear of what may be lurking beyond the entrance of the cave, Tank and I stand and stare at Genius. Finally, Tank says, "This rope doesn't look too sturdy, man, are you sure…"

Before Genius can answer, I chime in and say, "Genius, I don't think it's—"

He cuts me off before I finish my sentence. Pointing to the entrance, he says, "Shacoo, you stay right here and watch me as I progress. If anything happens, you shout for Tank to start pulling."

"I don't know, I think we should get—"

"Relax," Genius says in a brave voice. "Tank is strong— that's why we call him Tank. The cave isn't very big and Tank can quickly pull me out if anything goes wrong."

I look at Tank, "What do you think?" I ask.

Tank shrugs and looks at me with resignation written across his face. "Guess since Genius is determined, we can give it a try."

✳

TANK TAKES UP HIS position. He wraps the rope around the tree and then around his waist. When he's situated, he says, "With the rope around my waist, I'll have better leverage if I need to start pulling."

Genius nods and turns to me. "Ready?" he asks.

I'm beginning to rethink my desire for an adventure and don't know if I'm up to the uncertainty that we may encounter in the darkness of the cave. My heart is pounding so loud I can hear the beats in my ears. I surmise Genius' bravado is more contrived than genuine. He gives the rope a tug, testing it to make sure it's snug around his waist. Apparently satisfied, he turns to me, smiles and moves slowly forward taking the first steps into the cave. I can track Genius' movements by following the flashlight beam. After a while, I relax a little as everything seems to be going smoothly, well, at least, for now. Then suddenly, I'm racked with fear when I hear Genius grunt and at the same time, hear Tank yell, "Hey, what's going on?" I look at Tank and then back into the cave. That's when I see the beam of the flashlight pointing straight up to the top of the cavern, and it's not moving.

"Genius!" I cry. No answer. I try again, "Genius!" Still no answer.

Tank is immediately at my side. "What happened?" he demands. "I felt the rope jerk and then all of the sudden it went tight."

"I do...don't kno...know," I stutter. I'm already moving hand-over-hand down the rope toward the flashlight beam. Tank is right behind me; we proceed with extreme caution.

As we get closer to the beam of light, Tank grabs my arm and shouts, "STOP!"

"Tank, you scared me half to death. What is it?"

"Can't you see it? We're getting close to the edge of a pit," he says.

"Oh, my gosh!" I say and jump back. "I see it now. You saved me from falling in."

"I know. Get behind me, I'm taking the lead," Tank says. He then drops to his hands and knees and motions for me to do the same. Tank slowly crawls forward toward the beam of the flashlight. He's feeling his way along with his hands and I follow him staying very close. We move at a snail's pace still holding onto the rope. When we finally reach the edge of the pit, we peer in. We're relieved to discover that it's only about ten feet deep and gasp as we see Genius lying flat on his back at the bottom.

I call out to Genius again but he's non-responsive. "Tank, what'll we do?" I ask, in a panic.

"Take it easy, Shacoo," Tank says. From the tone of his voice, my guess is he's as distressed as I am, but he's trying to suppress his anxiety. "I see Genius still has the rope tied around his waist," Tank says. "Do you think we can pull him out?"

"Don't know. If he's hurt, it wouldn't be wise for us to move him."

"Good point."

Tank looks around the cave as if seeking another solution, then looks at me and says, "I'm going down."

"But—" I begin to protest.

Tank cuts me off, "Since the rope is tied around the tree, I'm sure I can use it to get out." He peers over the edge of the pit, "I can descend hand-over-hand and walk myself down the side of the pit to the bottom. After I check Genius for injuries, I can pull myself out."

"But—"

"It's okay, Shacoo, my Boy Scout training wasn't for nothing. I earned my First Aid Badge and I'm qualified enough to determine how badly Genius is hurt."

"But—"

"If he isn't hurt too badly, we'll pull him out. Otherwise, we'll have to come up with a better plan. It's just that simple." Tank looks at me with probing eyes, "Okay?"

"Okay," I manage to say, finally accepting the fact that we probably have no other option. Then I ask, "Are you sure this rope is strong enough?" I hold it up to make my point. "It feels pretty flimsy to me."

"We're not climbing Mt. Everest," Tank says. "We'll be out before you know it."

✳

I HOLD MY BREATH as I watch Tank lower himself hand-over-hand down the rope. He has his feet braced against the side of the pit as he descends and is able to slowly walk downwards in sync with his hand movements. When he reaches the bottom of the pit, he picks up the flashlight and shines it over Genius from head to toe, looking for any sign of injury.

"Genius," I hear Tank say. "Can you hear me?"

Genius moans. When I hear him moan I lay down flat on my stomach and lean over the edge as far as I dare so that I can see and better hear what's happening. Now I can see Genius and I watch him move his arms ever so slightly. Relief swarms over me.

"Genius!" Tank says again, "can you hear me?"

"Tank? What happened, where are we?"

"You took a fall. We're at the bottom of a pit."

"Where's Shacoo?" Genius asks, as he tries to sit up.

Tank points the flashlight to where I'm watching and Genius looks up. "Hey, Shacoo," he says, trying to appear macho.

"Genius, are you hurt?" I ask.

Genius slowly moves his legs and arms. "Don't think I'm hurt, just a bit dazed from the fall is all."

"Let me help you up." Tank takes Genius' hands and pulls him to his feet. At first, Genius staggers but soon stabilizes.

"Think I'm okay," he says to Tank. "We should try to get outta here."

"My thoughts exactly," Tank responds. "This is the plan. We can go up the same way I came down by using the rope to climb up the side of the pit hand-over-hand just like we do at the rock wall at the gym. Besides, it's not that far up."

Genius looks up again and I detect uncertainty in his voice when he asks Tank, "Did any of your movie heroes escape certain death by walking up the side of a pit?"

"Only when they had to," Tank answers and grins at Genius. "It's one of the basic skills we learned in Boy Scouts."

Genius looks up again and replies, "Doesn't look too difficult and it sure beats staying down here."

"That's the spirit!" Tank says, reassuring Genius. "Since you appear to be a little woozy, I'll go first and then I can help pull you up when I reach the top."

Genius nods.

I'm holding tightly onto the rope and watch as Tank starts climbing up. When he's almost to the top, I feel the rope go slack and then it suddenly starts racing through my hands; apparently it had come loose from the tree. Everything happens so fast I don't have time to react and I'm helpless as I watch my end of the rope snake over the edge of the pit and disappear. I'm near panic when I hear Tank grunt when he hits bottom.

"TANK!" Genius shouts.

I creep up to the rim and look over into the pit. Tank is lying on the dirt floor with the rope coiled on top of him and Genius is kneeling beside him with the flashlight. I breathe a sigh when I hear Tank say, "I'm okay."

The seriousness of the situation pounces on me like a cat springing on an unsuspecting mouse. Now Genius, Tank and the rope are in the pit and I'm going to need help to get them out.

I look at my watch, its one-thirty. Leaning over the edge, I call down to the boys, "I'm going to get help…"

"NO! Wait, Shacoo," Genius says. "I have an idea. Tank's plan was a good one, we just didn't expect the rope to come untied from the tree. I'm going to throw the rope up, you grab it and you tie your end to the tree."

"Do you want to chance that again?" I ask.

"Yes. Just grab the rope when I heave it up."

Genius rears back and hurls the rope upwards. However, after multiple tries we determine the rope is too light and neither Genius nor Tank can throw it high enough to reach the top of the pit.

"It isn't working," I say. "It's getting late, so I'm going to get help."

"Where are you going?" Genius asks.

"Outside where I can get service so I can make a call." I pause, then add, "I'm going to call the Greens."

"Oh no," I hear Genius utter as I make my way toward the light at the entrance of the cave.

✳

A RIVAL CLUB BY the name of Gang Green, or the Greens as the R*U*1*2s call them, lives on the other side of town. On several occasions when the R*U*1*2s have needed their help, they have come to our rescue. Bonz, the leader of the Greens, enjoys having the R*U*1*2s and especially Genius, at his mercy. Bonz is rarely seen out in public without two of his loyal sidekicks, Spyder and Bruiser.

Now that I'm out of the cave and have service for my cellphone, I punch in Bonz' number.

"Bonz," he answers.

"Bonz, it's Shacoo," I say.

"Shacoo, long time no talk!" Bonz says and before I can say more, he asks, "What kind of trouble is Genius in this time?"

I cringe. Bonz can be very abrasive. However, I conclude now is not the time to kibitz with him, so I don't waste words. I just tell him exactly what has happened and where we are—all except the part about the treasure. Then I plead with him, "Will you and the other Greens come help get Genius and Tank out of the pit? Please!"

"Sure, we'll help, but what the heck were you guys doing poking around up there anyway?"

I'm trapped. I don't see any other way to explain our actions except to tell Bonz about the treasure. And when I finish, Bonz says, "Well, why didn't you say so in the first place? After our rescue mission, we can help you search for the loot."

"Of course," I say, sorry I told him about the treasure.

"Spyder and Bruiser are here with me. We'll be there as soon as possible." After a pause, Bonz asks, "What do you think we'll need for the rescue?"

I think for a minute, "The pit is approximately ten feet deep. If our rope hadn't come untied, Tank's plan would have worked. So I guess we'll probably need some heavy rope and flashlights or lanterns."

"Okay, we can do that. That's the kind of stuff we keep on hand. Anything else—like an armored truck to load the treasure in?" Bonz says and laughs. I can hear Spyder and Bruiser laughing with him in the background.

I ignore Bonz' comment and say, "We parked our bikes close to the steps leading to the Sleeping Giant. I'll wait for you there."

"We're on our way."

After I end the call, I retrace my steps and go back into the cave. The boys have the flashlight on and I use the beam of light as a beacon to find my way to the pit. When they hear me approach, Tank calls out. "Shacoo, what's going on?"

"Bonz, Spyder and Bruiser are on their way," I say. "It'll probably take them at least a half hour to forty-five minutes—even though they have mountain bikes and can ride faster than we did."

"Was Bonz civil?" Genius asks.

"Yes, he was. He agreed to come help even before I told him about the treasure."

"You told him about the treasure?"

"I had to when he asked what we were doing up here."

"Oh, great!" Genius says.

I don't like Genius' tone of voice so I say, "And how else was I going to explain, on the spur of the moment, what we're doing here, looking for fossils?"

"Sorry, Shacoo," Genius says. "I guess I'm at the end of my rope."

"In more ways than one," I say. Only Tank and I laugh.

"I'm going back to where we left our bikes and wait for the Greens," I say. "You guys stay put, we'll be back as soon as possible."

"Stay put!" Tank snickers and adds, "Now everyone's a comedian. I only hope we get out of here before it gets dark."

"Now *that's* what I call funny, Tank," Genius snorts. "How much darker can it get?"

"I meant outside. I don't want our parents worried and I sure don't want to have to explain to them what we've been doing."

"Excellent observation," Genius says. "I apologize for my rudeness."

"Quite all right," Tank says. "After all, you're at the end of your rope."

JUDITH BLEVINS & CARROLL MULTZ •

"If the truth were known, we all are!" I say and walk in the direction of the bicycles.

✴

I'M ELATED WHEN I hear the clatter as the Greens approach my location. As soon as they come into view, I jump up and greet them. "Over here," I shout and wave my arms in the air.

"Hey, Shacoo," Spyder yells in a loud voice.

"You guys sure picked a hot day to get in a jam," Bonz says as he comes to a stop next to where I'm standing.

"Trust me, it wasn't planned to happen this way," I say.

"Never is…" Bruiser says. "You guys have a way of attracting disaster, kinda like moths to a flame."

"Okay, now that you've got your jabs in, can we get on with the rescue?" I say and look up at the sky. "It's going to be dark in a couple of hours."

"Sure," Bonz says. Then with a wry grin he adds, "Take me to your leader." Spyder and Bruiser break out in laughter appreciating *their* leader's sense of humor.

As the Greens secure their bicycles, I notice they have with them a large coil of rope and three camp lanterns. Once they're situated, Bonz says, "Okay, we're good to go. Let's get on with it."

I take the lead and we skirt the perimeter of the Sleeping Giant and head toward the cave. When we approach the entrance, I call out, "Genius, Tank, the Greens are here and we'll have you out in no time."

"That's good news," Tank responds, "our flashlight batteries are getting weak."

"Hey, you guys, you 'fraid of the dark?" Bruiser snickers.

"No, just of what crawls around in the dark," Genius shoots back.

"Knock off the chatter," Bonz orders, "and get those lanterns lit."

When the three lanterns are lit, they shed enough light for us to see our surroundings. I'm surprised that the cave is much larger than I originally thought. As I look around, I spot a rock outcropping about three feet from the ceiling just a few yards beyond the pit where Genius and Tank are trapped. It looks very much like the rock ledge I'd imagined.

The Greens have now lowered their rope into the pit. I listen as Bonz gives instructions to his followers as well as to Genius and Tank.

"Lighten up and pay attention!" he says, looking down at Genius and Tank. "Tie the rope 'round your waist—one at a time. When you give the signal we'll start pulling you out. Spyder, Bruiser and me are gonna be outside. We're going to use the tree as a pulley by wrapping the rope around its trunk. That way, the three of us will provide the manpower to raise you by us just walkin' forward." Bonz then asks, "*Capeesh?*"

"Yeah, we *capeesh*. And we're ready. Genius is coming out first," Tank says.

Bonz signals to Spyder and Bruiser to follow him. As they walk toward the entrance of the cave, Bonz says, "Okay. Shacoo, you stay right where you are. When Genius signals he's ready, relay the information to us. Don't go near the rim, we don't need another $R*U*1*2$ in the pit. We'll get 'em out."

I nod.

"Let's get to it then," Bonz says. "Come on you guys…"

The Greens take the rope, slowly uncoiling it as they leave the cave. I observe them from my position and watch as they wrap the rope around the tree. The three of them line up one behind the other and take a tight hold on the rope with both hands. "Give Bonz the signal," Genius shouts. "I'm ready!"

I wave to Bonz and call out to Genius, "We're ready on this end! Start your ascent."

"Okay, here I come," Genius calls back.

I watch the rope slowly move toward where the Greens are tugging on it as Genius slowly ascends from the pit.

Soon I see Genius' head appear above the rim of the pit. "Bonz, his head is above the rim," I shout.

"Okay!" Bonz calls back. "Tell him that we're going to keep pulling until he is completely out. It may be uncomfortable when we drag him forward across the dirt edge of the cave, but he needs to hang on tight until his legs are completely out."

"Yeah, we don't need him falling back into the dungeon," Bruiser smirks.

I bite my lip and ignore Bruiser's remark. After all, they did give up an afternoon to help and the least I can do is be cordial to them. After more tugging, Genius clears the pit.

I rush to where he lays face down, sprawled out on the ground. "Genius! I was so worried about you…"

He raises his head and manages a smile, "Hi, Shacoo," he says.

"Okay, cut the chit-chat and untie the rope and lower it down to Tank," Bonz barks.

Genius is already untying the rope as Bonz speaks. He crawls to the rim of the pit, "Tank, I'm sending the rope down. Tie it around your waist and let us know when you're ready."

"Okay." Tank says.

"I'm going to help the Greens pull Tank out," Genius says. "Shacoo, you stay here and make sure all goes as planned."

"But…but I thought you were hurt."

"Naw, just bumped my head when I fell and was dazed for a while. I'm fine now."

With the interior of the cave lit by the lanterns the Greens provided, Genius exclaims, "Do you see what I see?" He points to the rock outcropping I observed earlier.

Before I can answer Tank calls up to us, "I'm ready! Get me outta here!"

"I'll let the Greens know," Genius says and moves toward the entrance of the cave. In a matter of minutes, Tank, too, is topside. When the rescue is complete, we all gather outside the cave. I look at my watch, it's four-twenty.

"Oh, my gosh! We need to get going," I say.

Genius and Tank echo my sentiment.

Genius extends his hand to Bonz, and says, "Thanks, man. Maybe someday we can repay the favor."

Bonz gives Genius a knuckle bump. "Our mission is to serve and protect," he says. "And hopefully, we'll never be that desperate."

"That would be my hope, as well," Genius says, "but you never know."

"Right! You never know," Bonz replies.

Bonz and Bruiser go back into the cave and retrieve the lanterns and Spyder coils the rope as the Greens prepare to leave.

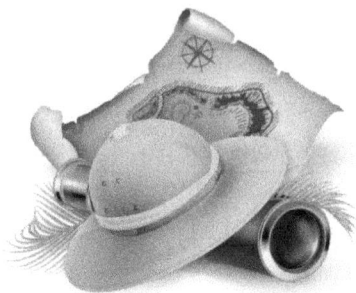

CHAPTER SIX
THE CURSE OF THE CAVE

efore the Greens leave and since I had to let them in on our secret, we all agree to meet at the cave early the next morning to continue the treasure hunt. When we leave the chamber, I notice that the sun has already begun to set.

"Oh, my gosh! We've got to get a move on," I say.

I watch Tank and Genius as they look up at the sky obviously realizing we're running out of time. We thank the Greens again and the three of us race to where our bicycles are parked. The Greens are still lingering by the cave site when we begin our ride down the mesa. Because they're older and allowed more freedom, they apparently are not worried about getting home before dark. About half-way down the mesa, Genius stops and signals us to do likewise.

"What's up, man?" Tank asks.

"Not sure. I notice the Greens haven't started down yet."

"I know," I say, and look back. "What do you think?"

"I don't want to believe what I'm thinking," Genius replies.

"That the Greens are going to go back to the cave and look for the treasure?" Tank says more in the form of a statement than a question.

"Precisely! Or at least that's my take," Genius replies.

"Now all the pieces fit. No wonder they were so eager to help us," I blurt. "Those slimy crooks!"

Genius shakes his head. "We have no choice but to move on so as not cause our parents any unnecessary worry."

I nod. "Or to get ourselves grounded."

"Why, I'd like to go back there and give 'em a piece of my mind…" Tanks sputters as he clenches his fists.

"Not worth it," I say. "Genius is right, we need to get home."

✳

WE LEARNED LATER THAT as soon as we left, the Greens went back into the cave. According to a friend of a friend, the following conversation between the three Greens ensued:

"This place is beginning to give me the creeps," Bruiser apparently mumbled.

"Sissy-man! Bet you're 'fraid of your own shadow," Spyder retorted.

"Knock it off, you two, and get the lanterns lit again. We ain't got all night!" Bonz snapped.

As the sun dropped lower in the western sky and the trees cast dark and mysterious shadows, Spyder handed one of the lanterns to Bonz, and asked, "How'd you know where to search?"

"I'm very observant, as you well know," Bonz replied. "Before we all left the cave, I watched the goodie two shoes stare up at a rock outcropping close to the ceiling of the cavern. And my friend, that's how I know." After a pause, Bonz reportedly added, "Maybe we can find Shacoo's treasure and keep the *R*U*1*2s* from falling victim to more disasters. Next time they may not be so lucky. At this rate, we can't spend the rest of the summer coming to their rescue. And if we do find something, they may give us a reward."

"You really think there's something up there?" Bruiser asked as he accepted the second lantern from Spyder.

"Only one way to find out," Bonz said, as he started back into the cave.

"Wait!" Bruiser said. "Even so, how do you expect to get up there?" and he pointed to the rock outcropping.

"Not me," Bonz replied, "you!"

"ME?"

"Sure. We'll lasso the outcropping with the rope and you can shimmy up it—just like the Navy Seals."

"Right, easy for you to say," Bruiser retorted.

"Come on, man!" Spyder interjected, "Where's your sense of adventure. Just think, you'll be the first to see the gold and silver coins cascading out of the treasure chest."

"Yeah! Didn't think of that," Bruiser said.

"Well then, let's get to it," Bonz said, as he began to uncoil the rope.

Maybe it's because of his questionable after-dark projects that Spyder displayed an uncanny ability with the rope and lassoed the outcropping on the first try. He tested the rope by tugging on it a few times, and as soon as he was satisfied the rope was secure, he pointed to Bruiser.

"Okay, Bruiser, make like a monkey and climb that banana tree."

"Very funny," Bruiser said, squinting at the setup. "You'll be laughing out the other side of your mouth begging for me to toss you a *banana*."

"Shut up, you two," Bonz chastised. "We've got work to do, now get going."

Bruiser grabbed the rope and began to shimmy up hand-over-hand. When he reached the rock outcropping he twisted the rope around one leg for additional security and boosted himself up high enough to grab onto the rock ledge.

The ledge was slick and Bruiser lost his handhold and toppled over backward. Fortunately, the rope he had twisted around his leg kept him from falling head first onto the cavern floor. But now Bruiser, it is told, was stuck suspended in midair, swinging back and forth upside down like a circus performer. Spyder grabbed the rope and stopped it from swinging.

"Thanks, man. Getting pretty dizzy."

Spyder looked at Bonz and asked, "Now what?"

"Give me a minute, will ya?" Bonz replied.

"I have an idea," Bruiser called down to them. "You give the rope a little slack so that I can wiggle my leg free and then I can just slide down."

Unable to come up with a solution of his own, Bonz said, "Okay, it's worth a try."

After a couple of attempts to get untangled, Bruiser finally was able to free his leg and slide down the rope. Other than a few bumps and scrapes, he was unhurt.

"Now what?" Bruiser asked as he stood and brushed the dirt from his tattered jeans and examined the scrapes on his knees.

Bonz looked up at the rope still lassoed around the outcropping. "Did you see anything up there before you fell?"

"Naw. I fell before I even had a chance and besides, it was too dark to see anything."

"We need a ladder," Spyder suggested.

"That's obvious, Sherlock. How do you propose we get a ladder up here—especially now that's it's getting dark?" Bruiser asked.

"Not gonna happen tonight," Spyder answered.

"Exactly!" Bonz said. "Guess we better abort and go home and meet back here tomorrow as we planned. I'm eager to see what the R*U*1*2s come up with. Spyder, get that rope down."

⊛

ON THE WAY HOME the afternoon before, Genius, Tank and I agree to the same arrangement we had that day. Genius would bring water, I would bring PBJ sandwiches, including enough for the Greens and Tank would bring a better rope. We would each bring a flashlight with fresh batteries.

⊛

"THINK THE GREENS WILL show up?" I ask as we gather in front of Genius' house.

"Depends on how their search without us went yesterday afternoon," Genius answers. "Guess we'll find out soon enough."

When we meet the Greens on Sleeping Giant Mesa, we're somewhat surprised they even showed up, and with a ladder, no less.

Guess they didn't find the treasure after all.

"How'd you get those up here?" Genius asks, pointing to the sections of ladder scattered on the ground before them.

"It wasn't easy! The ladder comes apart and we each carried a section," Bruiser says. "It's aluminum so it ain't heavy, just awkward."

"By the looks of you," Tank says, "you guys must have had a rough time getting home last evening."

I notice the Greens ignore Tank's remark. Tank and Genius look at me. I suspect I know what they're thinking.

"What happened to Bruiser? He's sure banged up," Genius says.

"Yeah. He took a tumble on the way down the mesa," Bonz says. "What's with the interrogation anyways? We gonna do this or not?"

"Yes, yes we are, so let's get going," I say.

THE GREENS LEFT THE lanterns in the cave the night before. When we enter, Spyder lights the lanterns and we all stare up at the rock outcropping.

"Is that where we're goin'?" Bonz asks, pointing to the rock outcropping.

I suspect he knows exactly where we're going and is just playing dumb. Otherwise, how would they know to bring a ladder?

"Yes. How intuitive of you to bring a ladder," I taunt.

"Huh! Oh, that. Well, we brought it just in case we needed one. You guys have a habit of falling into pits," Bonz says. Spyder and Bruiser laugh at Bonz' joke; Tank and Genius don't.

Tank and Bruiser assemble the ladder and when they're finished putting it together, they place it against the rock outcropping.

"I want to go first," I say. "After all, it is my inheritance."

"Sure, no problem," Bonz says.

It's obvious that the Greens were in here after we left yesterday and I don't like the way they're trying to take over. All the boys stand in a semicircle at the bottom of the ladder holding it as I ascend. I have my flashlight in my hip pocket, so when I reach the top, I steady myself on the top rung of the ladder and retrieve the flashlight from my pocket. Shining my light into a shallow crevice located above the outcropping, I survey the floor, ceiling and walls.

"I don't see anything," I say.

"Are you sure," Bonz says. "Come on down and let me take a look."

"Okay," I say.

When I reach the bottom of the ladder, Bonz steps up and borrowing my flashlight, he climbs up to the outcropping. We watch as he ascends and when he reaches the top rung he leans all of his weight forward on the rock ledge and with my flashlight in one hand and the other hand on the ladder, he swivels his head back and forth looking around.

"Shacoo's right," Bonz says. "There's nothing up here. I'm coming down."

"Wild goose chase," Spyder says. "Too bad. Wonder if someone beat us to it?"

Someone like you, maybe.

"Well, thanks for your help, anyway," I say.

Bonz has just barely started his descent when we hear a cracking sound. When we look up, we watch the rock outcropping as it begins to crumble. Pieces of rock cascade around us.

"What the…" Bonz cries out. Apparently realizing what's happening, he grabs the sides of the ladder with his hands and puts his feet on the outside of the rungs and slides down the ladder in typical fireman fashion. He lands on his feet and as soon as he's steady, all of us rush out of the cave, just in the nick of time. The rock outcropping has completely come loose from the wall of the cavern and falls in a heap to the floor.

"Jumpin' Jupiter, that was close," Spyder says, as he watches Bonz looking for injuries he may have received from his brush with disaster.

"I'm okay," Bonz mumbles as Spyder helps him brush the dust and debris from his jeans and T-shirt. "But I don't believe in coincidences," he says. "This place is cursed and I don't want anything more to do with it."

We all stare at Bonz for a few awkward moments. Guess the others are just as stunned as I am that Bonz believes in things like curses.

Finally, Bruiser asks, "What about the ladder and lanterns?"

"Leave 'em. They're buried under the rubble anyways," Bonz retorts.

I'm grateful to the Greens and I want them to know it so I say, "I brought some sandwiches. Would you like one before you go?"

"What kind?" Bruiser asks.

Before I can answer, Bonz signals his sidekicks to fall in as he heads for the bikes. "Naw, we gotta get going," he says. "Better luck next time." Before they're out of sight, Bonz turns back and calls out to us, "You'd be smart to abort this little escapade. This place is obviously cursed."

Bonz' statement makes me cringe. He may have a valid point. *Wonder if something else happened to them after we left last evening?*

✳

GENIUS, TANK AND I begin to gather up the items we had left on the outside of the cave as we prepare to start for home. Before I secure my flashlight in my backpack, I shine it into the cave for one last look. When I do, I see something glistening in the light and I grab Genius' arm.

"Look!" I shout and point toward the object that is reflecting the light.

Genius stops and crouches down following the beam of light. "By Jove, Shacoo. I do see something shining in the light." Genius stands and says, "You two wait here. I'm going to investigate."

"Oh, I don't know. After all the bad luck we've experienced, I—"

Before I can finish my sentence, Genius reassures me that it's all right. "The sought-after object is only a short distance from the entrance. I can be in and out in less than a minute. Don't worry."

I hear Tank sigh as he joins me. He takes my hand and I cringe as we watch Genius gingerly move into the cave with my flashlight in hand. Afraid to continue watching, I squeeze my eyes closed. In a matter of minutes, Genius is back and hands me a small tin box similar to the one I found in the trunk in Grandpa Tomaso's attic.

"There *was* a treasure!" I squeal.

"Wow!" Tank exclaims. "Come on, let's have a look."

I'm fumbling around trying to pry the lid open when Genius says, "Here, let me do it!"

I reluctantly hand him the tin. After a number of tries, Genius is also unable to open it.

"Can I try?" Tank asks.

"Sure," I say and Genius hands him the tin.

Tank has it open in less than ten seconds and hands it back to me. Genius looks at him with a bewildered expression on his face.

"You guys had it loosened, I just squeezed and it opened right up," Tank says.

I think Tank's response was intended to keep Genius from feeling inadequate. That proves to me that Tank values Genius' friendship more than he values praise.

When I take the tin from Tank, my hands are shaking. "Come on, Shacoo," Genius prompts, "Let's see what's in there!"

I remove a tightly folded piece of paper from the box. It appears to be pretty fragile. I'm fearful if I try to unfold it, it will crumble. I look to Genius for help.

"After all of the calamity," Genius says, "my knees are weak. Let's go sit down in the shade of the trees and see what we have here."

We sit down in a circle and Tank and I look at Genius waiting for him to unfold the fragile looking piece of paper. Genius lays the paper on a large flat rock and very carefully smooths the creases as he unfolds them one-by-one. He treats the paper as gentle as he would a newborn kitten. Tank quietly sits next to him, apparently mesmerized at the prospect of what the paper has to reveal. When at last the paper is completely unfolded, Genius looks at me and says, "It appears to be in the same handwriting as the journal."

"Yes," I reply, "I noticed that. What does it say?"

Genius reads aloud the contents of the note.

April 16, 1935

If you find this, you figure out code in journal. I not trust bank because of crash in 1929. I bury fortune and make map for you, whoever you are. Map in tin box will lead to buried treasure.

Today my 80 birthday. My love, Maria, not here. She go to be with God in heaven 2 year ago. Before she leave me, she tell me to put her heirloom

ruby ring her mama gave her with money when
I hide box. Ring very special to her. She want to
keep ring in family and she fear some stranger
will steal it.

We sit for a few minutes pondering the hidden meaning of
the note. "What do you think?" I finally ask.

Genius answers, "Apparently your ancestor lost faith in the
banking system when many banks failed. On October 29, 1929,
better known as Black Tuesday, according to Ms. Forester, the
New York Stock Exchange completely collapsed, causing a run
on the banks. She attributed the collapse of the stock market as
the primary factor in causing the Great Depression."

"What does a run on the banks mean?" Tank asks.

Genius scratches his head, apparently thinking of how to
word his explanation. He finally says, "A run means that large
numbers of people, during that period, withdrew all their money from the banks which led to many bank failures. I remember Ms. Forester telling our social studies class that, probably
as a result of the crash of '29, many people during that era were
antsy about putting their hard-earned money into banks because there was no guarantee they could withdraw it later. This
uncertainty led to the establishment of the FDIC. That's when
President Roosevelt signed the 1933 Banking Act into law. You
may have seen the initials FDIC painted on the bank windows.
The acronym, FDIC, stands for Federal Deposit Insurance
Corporation. The initial Act insured that investors' deposits of
up to two thousand five hundred dollars would be covered by
the government if the bank failed." I notice a thoughtful look
cross Genius' face before he adds, "Today, the FDIC insures up
to two hundred fifty thousand dollars. That's a hundred times
more than it was in 1933.

"What that means, is if you lose more than the amount the FDIC insures, you will only get up to what the FDIC insures. That's why corporations and well-to-do individuals spread their deposits around in multiple banks. The FDIC only cares about how much you have deposited in a single bank. In other words, you are entitled to receive up to two hundred fifty thousand dollars in each of the failing banks you have with active accounts.

"If Shacoo's treasure is one or two thousand dollars, it's still only worth one or two thousand dollars because it wasn't invested and earning interest. However, it's interesting to note that one thousand dollars in 1929 would be equal to fourteen thousand dollars' worth of buying power in today's world. In other words, it would take fourteen dollars today to buy what one dollar would have bought in 1929."

Sitting there listening to the exchange, I'm completely mesmerized by Genius' vast knowledge of so many things.

Discouraged by the thought that the face value of the currency might be worth less today than it was when it was buried was soon replaced by the thought that old bills might be considered as antiques and have greater value. If the coins were gold or silver, they would be worth more today because the price of gold and silver has skyrocketed. In any event whatever the treasure consists of, it could be worth a fortune.

Apparently I smiled because Genius says, "Shacoo, you look like the cat that swallowed the canary. You know something we don't or are you making fun of me?"

When I tell him what I was mulling over in my mind, he says, "Guess we know who the brain is in this outfit!"

"I knew it all the time," I say. Genius and I both laugh. Tank just frowns.

"Where's your sense of humor?" Genius asks Tank.

"Sorry, I was wondering how Shacoo's great-great grandfather got that tin box up that high."

I was wondering the same thing.

"Good question," Genius replies. "I remember hearing something about a cave-in that occurred on Sleeping Giant Mesa many years ago."

"Of course! I remember Ms. Forester telling our geography class about major events that can change the topography of a landscape," Tank says. "She mentioned the near disaster at Dipsy Dam just last year and how a dam break could drastically change the terrain. She also said that some years ago there was a cave-in on Sleeping Giant Mesa that caused a major rock shift."

"I remember that. Ms. Forester said that she was particularly interested in informing us about things that affected us locally. Great-Great Grandpa Giovanni must have hid the tin box before the cave-in altered the area surrounding the cavern," I say. "Before the cave-in, there was probably easy access to where the tin box was hidden—also, we don't know who dug the pit and when. It could have been either Great-Great Grandpa Giovanni to keep the treasure from being discovered or treasure seekers hunting for the treasure."

"Maybe the main part of the treasure was found and the tin box is all that remains," Tank offers.

Genius nods but I can tell he is absorbed in studying the map. Finally, he says, "The map is easy to decipher. The treasure is not hidden on Sleeping Giant Mesa at all. If my hunch is correct, it's buried right under our noses."

I'm not sure what that means so I ask, "Exactly where is that?"

"I'm still working on that," Genius says. "Are we ready to leave?"

I look over at Tank and he nods.

"I think so and the sooner the better," I say.

Genius refolds the map, puts it back in the tin box and hands it to me. I tuck it into my pocket. I'm relieved that at least we don't have to go back into the cave. When I think of the near disasters we encountered, I shiver. Bonz was sure in a rush to leave after the rock shelf collapsed. I wonder if something else happened to them after we left that first evening. I don't want to say it out loud, but I agree with Bonz when he says the cave, including the treasure, is no doubt cursed.

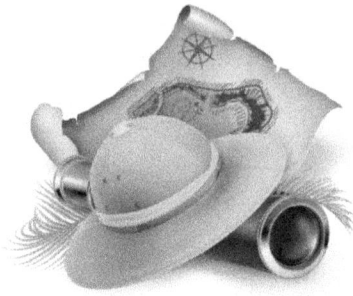

CHAPTER SEVEN

X MARKS THE SPOT

On the ride back to Jefferson City, Genius is silent and appears to be deep in thought. Tank and I recognize the signs that Genius is on another planet so we follow suit and keep our conversation to a minimum. When we're a couple of miles from town, Genius looks at me and asks, "Where did your great-great-grandparents live before they moved to what is now known as the ancestral home?"

I think for a moment, then say, "I believe they lived in a house provided to them by the city after Great-Great-Grandpa Giovanni was elected mayor. The house was on Globe or Maple, close to where Pearsons' orchard is located. It's since been razed and is part of Jefferson City Park. According to dad, it used to be the spot where the swimming pool sets."

"Hmmm. Do either of you know how long the orchard has been there?" Genius asks.

"For as long as I can remember, but I'm only twelve," I say.

"I know," Genius says, "I thought maybe one of you may have heard it mentioned at some time or another."

Tank shakes his head. "I think the orchard was there when the Pearsons bought the property. I heard that's why they bought it," he says. "Mr. Pearson was raised on a farm and they wanted to raise Sally in a smaller, more friendly community close to town."

"I remember hearing that also," I say. "They moved to Jefferson City just before Sally was born." Then it hits me as to why Genius is asking about the Pearson orchard, "You don't think by chance that that's where the treasure is buried, do you? It would have been close to where Great-Great Grandpa Giovanni lived."

"I'm pretty sure it is—and if my calculations are correct, it looks like it's buried under our old clubhouse, the one that used to be an apple storage shed," Genius says very matter of factly. "That's why I said it's probably buried right under our noses."

Tank and I stare open-mouthed at Genius. "Naw! You're kiddin'," Tank snorts.

"Not kidding," Genius replies.

I pull my bike to a stop. The boys do likewise. "Really?" I ask. "You're not kidding?"

"Really, not kidding. However, before we start digging like a pack of moles, I want to go to the Planning and Zoning Department to research the plat that corresponds to the orchard to make sure my theory is correct."

"I want to go to the planning office with you," I volunteer. "I think most county offices open at eight."

"Sure, you can help me research," Genius says.

Looking confused, Tank asks, "What's a plat?"

"A plat is a survey used to identify boundaries. It's the legal description of real estate," Genius says and motions for us to start riding again.

Falling in beside Genius, Tank asks, "Why do we need to know that? We already know where the clubhouse is."

"That's true, but I think we can use the plat to better pinpoint the place indicated with an X on the treasure map." Genius glances in Tank's direction, "Remember, we learned in our geography class that public information includes, among other things, property addresses, parcel maps and property characteristics. These are the factors that we're interested in, especially the parcel map. I'm pretty sure the apple shed or bunkhouse wasn't there when the map was made by Shacoo's ancestor. And I'm also pretty sure that we can't dig up the whole area in and around the clubhouse without causing a stir."

"Oh!" Tank says, apparently finally connecting the dots.

"You want to go with us?" Genius asks.

Looking pretty dejected, Tank says, "I promised my mom that I'd help her with the yard tomorrow, so I won't be able to go."

"Going to the planning office isn't that exciting. You won't be missing much," Genius says. "We'll catch up with you later."

THE NEXT MORNING GENIUS and I are at the Planning and Zoning Department at eight sharp.

"Well, hello, Shacoo," Jake Hellerman says.

Mr. Hellerman heads up the Planning and Zoning Department for Jefferson County. He is also one of my dad's golfing buddies. "What in the world brings you and your friend out this early in the morning?" he asks. "Surely, it can't be anything as boring as what the Planning and Zoning Department offers."

"Morning, Mr. Hellerman," I say. "Genius and I would like to look at a plat."

I watch him raise his eyebrows. "A plat? What on earth for? Are you *R*U*1*2s* planning on building something?"

"Ah, no. Well, you see, ah…" I stammer.

Genius comes to my rescue and says, "We're doing some research for a project we're working on."

"Hmmm, must be pretty technical," Mr. Hellerman replies. "Okay, come on around and I'll set you up at a desk."

As we round the counter, Mr. Hellerman asks, "Any specific area you want to research?"

"Yes," Genius says. "The area around Globe and Maple Streets."

"Globe and Maple," Mr. Hellerman says, as he runs his finger along the spines of a bank of three-ring binders. "You're the second person this month requesting information for that area."

I look at Genius. He just shrugs.

Mr. Hellerman pulls a binder from the bookshelf and thumbs through it. Having found the plat he was looking for, he spreads the notebook open on the desk in front of us. "There ya go," he says. "Most of this part of the plat encompasses the Pearson orchard. You can thumb through forward and backward if you're looking for anything specific."

"Thank you," Genius says. "This'll work just fine."

Mr. Hellerman nods and turns back to the front counter. "Let me know if you need anything else."

As soon as he's out of earshot, I say, "What do you make of that?"

"Of what?" Genius asks as he studies the plat.

"Someone else researching—"

"That's not unusual—happens all the time in the construction business. Builders need to make sure of the boundaries, easements, access roads, power lines and many other things before they break ground."

"Oh, guess I should have figured that out. I'm just anxious about the treasure after our experience with the Greens."

"Sure, I understand," Genius says. "Did you bring the map?"

"Of course. I have it right here." I take the tin box from my pocket and hand it to Genius.

Genius takes the map from the box and gently spreads it open on top of the plat. He begins to run his fingers across the plat and traces the map at the same time. After a few moments, he says, "I believe the old clubhouse is right here," and points to a spot located between Globe and Maple.

I'm not sure I understand all the markings on the plat, but I nod, trying to keep up with him.

"At the time your great-great-grandfather buried the treasure, the orchard was established but the old clubhouse, or as it was originally intended, the apple storage shed, was not yet built."

"But," I say, "the map must be close to one hundred years old. Do apple trees live that long?"

"Absolutely. In fact, one species, the Bramley, is known to have a life of over two hundred years. However the usual life expectancy for an apple tree is about one hundred years."

I nod again. I know from biology that trees produce one ring each year. The rings grow under the bark. When a tree falls or is cut down, you can determine its age by counting the rings exposed around its trunk. However, I had no idea apple trees could live a hundred years or longer.

Genius looks up at me. "That's one of life's little ironies, burying the treasure in the exact spot that, almost a century later, would later become the *R*U*1*2s'* clubhouse."

This is all surreal to me. I feel like I'm having a dream. "How can you tell where the treasure was buried from studying the plat?"

"By comparing the plat to the map," he says. "It's like measuring the distance from one place to another. Besides, it's the only place in the orchard where there's a rock formation."

Once again, I'm blown away by Genius' intuition and analytic ability even more than by the uncanny coincidence.

"I think we've got what we need," Genius says, as he closes the binder. "Let's go to the old clubhouse and put our theory to the test."

"Won't we need shovels?"

"Nope. We still have to figure out the exact spot, or as close to it as we can get."

Mr. Hellerman is standing at the front counter when we leave the Planning and Zoning Department. "Find what you were looking for?" he asks.

"Yes, we did," I say. "And thank you so much for your help."

"Not a problem, that's what we're here for. I actually enjoy it when the youth of our community take an interest in the workings of our local government." His attention is then redirected when an elderly man walks up to the counter. "You kids take care…and come back to see us again sometime."

"Thanks again," Genius says, and we leave the office.

Once outside, Genius pulls his cellphone from his hip pocket and calls Tank. "Tank, Genius here. Can you meet us at the clubhouse?"

"I'm still helping mom in the yard and don't think I can get away anytime soon. You find out anything at the planning department?"

"Yep! We lucked out and I think we got 'er pinpointed."

"That's great! What are you going to do now?"

"We're going to run by the old clubhouse and scope it out."

"Darn! Wish I could come too, but mom's project comes first. Keep me posted."

"Of course. And if it's any consolation, we won't be doing any digging today," Genius says and snickers, "We're saving that privilege until you can participate."

Tank laughs, "Sure—however, I think that's what you call saving the grunt work, not the privilege."

✳

AS SOON AS GENIUS ends the call, we head for the Pearson orchard and the old clubhouse. My heart flutters with anticipation at the thought of what we may discover buried there after all these years. And by his manner, I can tell Genius is as eager as I am to uncover the mystery. I also think about the location of the orchard's packing shed (our old clubhouse) and the anticipated location of the treasure. It is the most likely spot for both since it is one of the few barren, flat and isolated locations in the orchard. And in all likelihood, judging from the out-cropping of rock nearby, the treasure would be easy to locate at some later date.

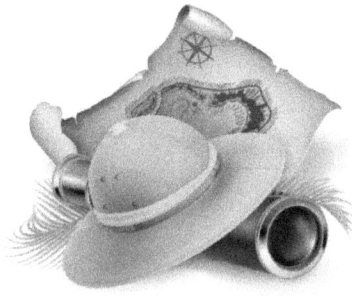

CHAPTER EIGHT

AW, SHUCKS!

As we approach the old clubhouse, we hear a lot of commotion. Getting closer, we see Mr. Pearson's orchard is buzzing with men in work clothes and hard hats. I look at Genius, "What do you think is going on?" I ask.

"Looks like Mr. Pearson is building something. I remember a cement mixer truck passing us when we made the turn at Maple. And that would explain why someone else was looking at the plat and probably getting a building permit."

I cringe. Suddenly anxiety swarms over me and I become concerned. "Oh, no! What if...what if...?

"Hold on, Shacoo. Let's just wait and see what's going on before we get caught up in the 'what ifs!'" Genius suggests.

Genius always takes the "let's be logical" stance. His statement did little to quell my fears. As we get near the old clubhouse site, we're stopped in the lane by one of the contractors who I recognize as Sam Larson.

"Whoa! Hold on there, young'uns," Mr. Larson says. "There's construction going on here and you're not allowed past this point."

"What construction is going on?" I blurt.

Sam takes off his hardhat and swipes his forearm across his brow. "Hot day," he says, and looks toward the spot where the clubhouse used to stand.

I follow his gaze and that's when I notice the old clubhouse is no longer there. My heart sinks and I feel tears welling up in my eyes.

Mr. Larson continues, "Mr. Pearson finally decided to tear down that old dilapidated apple shed and build a new one. It was a disaster waiting to happen with so many youngsters playing in and around the orchard."

"Oh, no!" I say.

"Hey, little lady. Don't take it so hard," Mr. Larson says. "I know the *R*U*1*2s* used the old structure as a clubhouse, but didn't Mr. Pearson gave you a nicer one—that old abandoned bunkhouse over on the other side of the orchard?"

"Yes, he did, and we're very grateful," Genius says, then he asks, "How far along is the construction on the new apple shed?"

Mr. Larson turns, and putting his hand on his utility belt, looks back toward the construction site. "We just finished pouring the cement for the floor…"

I'm so distraught that I don't hear the rest of what he is saying. There goes any hope of finding the treasure. It's probably covered by cement. Now we'll never know what it was. I can't control the tears and I begin to cry.

Mr. Larson looks at me with concern in his eyes. "Is she all right?" he asks Genius.

"Ah, yes, ah, she was just very attached to the old clubhouse. Sentimental value, you know. Kinda like losing an old friend."

"Yep, I do know what you mean. I have a teenage daughter that hangs onto everything. I may have to build an extra room onto our house to store the memorabilia she has been collecting over the years." Mr. Larson turns and looks back again. "Well, nice talking to you. I've got to get back on the job. Don' want to get fired, you know."

"It was nice talking to you, too. Thanks for the information," Genius says. We then turn our bikes around and head back down the lane and out of the orchard.

Genius must have noticed the tears streaming down my cheeks although I'm trying very hard to keep from crying.

"I'm sorry, Shacoo, and I'm disappointed, as well. It would have been fun to uncover something belonging to your ancestors. Even if it wasn't a fortune, it would still have been a treasure."

I nod. I'm unable to talk because I'm so emotional.

"At least it wasn't a total loss," Genius says. "You had a chance to get acquainted with Giovanni and Maria through reading the journal. You got a glimpse into their lives after they arrived in America. That's a personal touch and something very special that most people never get the opportunity to appreciate firsthand."

I keep peddling. "Thank you for being such a good friend," I say, and look over at Genius. He smiles at me. "I'll take the journal back to my grandparents tomorrow. Think I'll skip the details regarding our treasure hunt."

"Probably a good idea," Genius agrees.

⊛

WHEN I ARRIVE HOME, even though I'm exhausted, I immediately call Sally, remembering my promise to her.

Hi, Shacoo.

How nice to hear from you.

"Hi, Sally," I say. "If you're available, I'm free tomorrow."

Actually, I am,

What's the plan?

"Cookies are the plan. What time would you like to come over to help bake them?"

I can hear Sally conversing with her mother in the background. When she comes back on the line, she says:

Mommy said before three

I have to take a nap you see.

"How about two? That would give us enough time."

More conversation in the background. Then Sally comes back on the phone,

Two o'clock works just great

Then I won't get home too late.

"Okay. See you tomorrow," I say.

After I end the call, I go to my room and pull from under my bed the box that contains my assortment of precious objects. I open the lid and gaze at the items I've collected over the years and lovingly pick them up and examine them one-by-one. They consist of the following: the Snow White costume I wore on Halloween the autumn the *R*U*1*2s* nabbed *The Cat*, a burglar who had been terrorizing our neighborhood for months; the silver charm bracelet Genius gave me that was damaged at the time *The Weasel* kidnapped me from the Atkinson driveway when the *R*U*1*2s* were playing hide and seek; the newspaper clipping announcing the bestowing of U.S. citizenship on the little Cuban refugee we called *Blue*; the swatch of cloth Genius found on the widow's walk of Bradbury Mansion that was torn from Lucinda's ghostly gown; the magic wand that I confiscated from Sally after she used it to materialize Snow White and Little Red Riding Hood from her storybooks; tickets from the *Time Traveler* carnival ride that propelled Sally and me back in time to ancient Egypt, and Genius and Tank back in time to ancient Rome; and now, the tin box containing Great-Great-Grandpa Giovanni's treasure map; one that, it appears, will never reveal the secret it holds.

As I reflect on these items, memories return in vivid detail. I realize that Genius was right. The adventures I've shared with the *R*U*1*2s* mean more to me than any gold or silver or precious gems. I return my memory box to its sanctuary and stretch out on my bed, gazing at the ceiling.

I did find a treasure. Even though it isn't what I expected, it's just as precious all the same. True friendship can't be bought, only earned. And because of Genius, Tank and my many other friends, I feel like I'm a very rich girl, rich in what really matters in life. Where our heart is, there resides our treasure.

SALLY SHOULD BE HERE any minute. I glance at the clock as I assemble the items needed for making the cookie dough. I have a small step stool that I pull up to the counter for Sally to stand on. Our routine is that I measure out the ingredients and Sally adds them into the mixing bowl one at a time. After I stir the ingredients into dough, Sally and I form it into small balls and place the balls on a cookie sheet. I put them in the oven and together we clean up the mess while we wait for the cookies to bake. I look out of the window and see Sally coming up the walk, so I hurry to open the door for her. "Come on in, Sally. We're ready to start."

Hi, Shacoo,

What can I do?

"Nothing, Sally, except your part," I say as I tie an apron around Sally's waist and help her up on the stool. As we're mixing the dough, Sally says,

Daddy tore the old clubhouse down,

And you'll never guess what they found

When they dug up the old dirt floor—

I stop stirring and grab Sally's hand. "Wait! Don't tell me, I think I know."

No, Shacoo, it's not a game, it's for sure,

Treasure was hidden under the floor.

"Was it a tin box with a ruby ring?" I ask.

Sally has a surprised expression on her face and says,

Yes it was, how'd …how'd you guess?

How'd you know what was hidden in that mess?

"Well, you see when I went to my grandparents' house last week, I found a treasure map in an old family journal in the attic. It led us to the old clubhouse. However, we were too late. The cement had already been poured so we couldn't dig for the treasure."

I see. Shucks, now I don't know what to do,

The treasure must really belong to you.

"I don't know, Sally. We need to talk to your father. After all, it was buried on his property."

When we finish baking the cookies, I walk Sally home. Her father is mowing the lawn when we get there. "My two favorite girls, Sally and Shacoo," he says as we approach. "What have you been up to?"

Rhymin' must run in the family! "Good afternoon, Mr. P," I say. "If you have a minute, we have something we need to discuss with you."

"Sure, I always have time for Sally and her friends," he replies. He then wipes his brow with his handkerchief and motions for us to join him on the porch. "What's in that plastic bag you're carrying, Sally…as if I didn't know. I could smell cookies a block away."

Sally hands the bag to her father and sits down on the top step. We join her.

"You look so serious, what's the problem?" Sally's father asks as he opens the cookie bag and makes a selection.

Sally looks at me with her big blue eyes,

> *You explain to Daddy, Shacoo.*
> *You do it better than I do.*

"I'm really curious," Sally's father says. "And I'm all ears…"

When I finish my narrative, Sally's father takes off his baseball cap and runs his hands through his hair. "That's quite a story," he says, "and I agree with Sally that the treasure is rightfully yours." He stands and says, "Come on in."

When we enter the house, Sally's mother joins us.

"Bring the metal box with the ring the workers found in the excavation. Apparently it is an heirloom that belongs to the Bandaris'," Mr. P says to Sally's mother.

Mrs. P leaves the room, and when she returns, she hands the box to Sally's father. It is similar to the small metal box that contained the map. I'm surprised by its size. I guess I expected a large chest with a lot of gold and silver and really much more.

The metal box being rusted, quickly yields to Mr. P's prying. Inside Mr. P retrieves a ring box that is in surprisingly good condition. Opening the lid of the ring box, Mr. P retrieves a small ruby ring and sticks it on the end of the little finger of his right hand. "Wish it fit me," Mr. P says as he displays it before me. The ruby is rather large and glistens in the light as if it just came from the jewelers. The same is true of the gold upon which it is mounted. The ring seems to hold something mystical as my eyes are transfixed on it.

As Mr. P extends the finger with the ring, it suddenly slips off. "That's funny," he says as he leans over and picks up the ring. "As tight as it was, I can't believe it slipped off."

When Mr. P slips the ring all the way back onto his little finger, it fits perfectly. I'll never forget the surprised look on his face. "Either my finger shrank, or the ring grew," he says as he slips the ring on and off his finger.

It was then I remembered one of the entries in the journal that intimated that the ring had magical powers. "Mr. P, I blurt, "the possessor of the ring has magical powers."

"Yes, but…" Mr. P still seems stunned and at a loss to offer an explanation.

"While you held the ring, you *wished* it would fit," I add. "Your wish was granted."

"That's stuff for fairy tales," Mr. P says as he continues manipulating the ring.

"Yet…" Mrs. P says as she squints over her glasses at her husband.

Now Sally is at her father's side, reaching for the ring.

> *I've always wanted a puppy for a pet.*
> *I still don't have one yet.*
> *If the ring is really magic*
> *It will be a very handy gadget.*

"Sally," Mr. P. pleads, "some things you have are for fun—like your magic wand."

> *Daddy, please you don't know for sure*
> *The magic ring could cause quite a stir.*
> *If it worked for you, it'll work for me,*
> *Please, I need to try it don't you see?*

"Sally, you're impossible. Take the ring and do your thing."
Now I know from what side of the family Sally learned her rhymin' ways.
Sally closes her eyes and holding the ruby ring says,

> *I wish, I wish, oh how I wish*
> *I had a puppy named Trish.*

When Sally opened her eyes and no puppy by the name of Trish or otherwise stood before her, she pouted and handed the ring back to her father. It was at that moment the doorbell rang and the next-door neighbor entered carrying a small puppy.

"It's for Sally," Mrs. Carlson said as she handed the puppy to Sally. "Roxy had puppies and Trish is the only one left of the litter."

We were all stunned even though I was fairly well convinced the ring had such powers.

"It's an uncanny coincidence—plain and simple," Mr. P says shrugging . As he starts to hand the ring to me, Mrs. P says, "Homer, before you give the ring to Shacoo, let me have it for just a moment. Remember, Jefferson City Community Hospital is short a hundred thousand dollars of its goal to add a children's wing. Just for fun, let me make a wish that the hospital receives the much-needed funds by noon tomorrow." After she makes the wish, she hands me the ring.

Several days later, my father read to my mother a newspaper account that announced that an anonymous donor had provided a gift in the amount of one hundred thousand dollars to Jefferson City Community Hospital. The children's wing could now become a reality.

⊕

WHEN I TRY TO give the ruby ring to my Grandpa Bandaris, he says, "Shacoo, I promised the ring or whatever treasure you found would be yours. You're old enough to know that power not held in check can not only accomplish good but evil as well. In the wrong hands it could spell the end of civilization as we know it. Much like the Holy Grail, those seeking it might stop at nothing to obtain it. With that in mind, you might consider it a lucky charm but in reality it might be a curse in disguise. Don't tempt destiny."

Although I still have the ruby ring, I'm careful who I show it to. Only Genius, my family and Sally's have been made aware of its power. Although I have vowed never to use it, I've been tempted once or twice. What will become of it? I still haven't decided. Perhaps someday, one of the readers of my account will come up with a suggestion that will truly advance the best interest of humankind. Until then, it will be safely tucked away in the old tin box in which it was placed lo! those many years ago.

THE R*U*1*2 GANG GOES ON THEIR
MOST DANGEROUS ADVENTURE YET!
AND IT NEEDS TWO WHOLE BOOKS TO TELL IT!

SUMMER VACATION

PART ONE: CASTAWAYS

BY JUDITH BLEVINS
& CARROLL MULTZ

COMING SOON!

ABOUT THE AUTHORS

Judith Blevins' whole professional life has been centered in and around the courts and the criminal justice system. Her experience in having been a court clerk and having served under five consecutive district attorneys in Grand Junction, Colorado, has provided the fodder for her novels. She has had a daily dose of mystery, intrigue and courtroom drama over the years and her novels share all with her readers. In addition to the novels in The Childhood Legends Series®, she has authored or coauthored nine adult novels.

Carroll Multz, a trial lawyer for over forty years, a former two-term district attorney, assistant attorney general, and judge, has been involved in cases ranging from municipal courts to and including the United States Supreme Court. His high profile cases have been reported in the *New York Times, Redbook Magazine* and various police magazines. He was one of the attorneys in the *Columbine Copycat Case* that occurred in Fort Collins, Colorado, in 2001 that was featured by Barbara Walters on *ABC's 20/20*. Now retired, he is an Adjunct Professor at Colorado Mesa University in Grand Junction, Colorado, teaching law-related courses at both the graduate and undergraduate levels. In addition to the novels in the The Childhood Legends Series®, he has authored or coauthored eleven adult novels and seven books of non-fiction.

THE CHILDHOOD LEGENDS® SERIES

BY JUDITH BLEVINS & CARROLL MULTZ

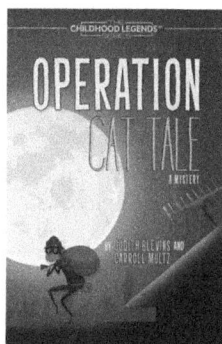

OPERATION CAT TALE

ONE FRIGHTFUL DAY

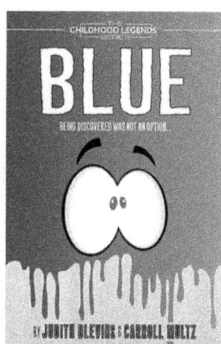

BLUE

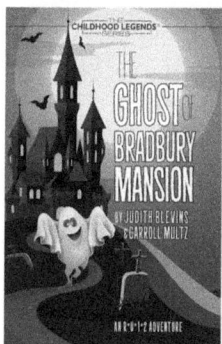

THE GHOST OF BRADBURY MANSION

WHITE OUT

A FLASH OF RED

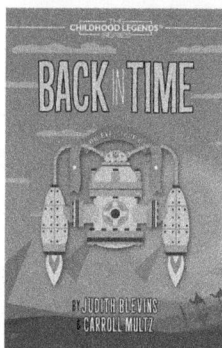

BACK IN TIME

THE ENTIRE R*U*1*2 COLLECTION IS AVAILABLE IN SOFTCOVER & EBOOK
AT BOOKSELLERS EVERYWHERE

CPSIA information can be obtained
at www.ICGtesting.com
Printed in the USA
FSHW01n0217070918